25¢

Disney

Minnie Mysteries

The Flower Prowler

Random House 🏠 New York

Copyright © 1997, 1998, 2004 Disney Enterprises, Inc. All rights reserved under International and Pan-American Copyright Conventions.
Published in the United States by Random House Children's Books, a division of Random House, Inc., New York, and simultaneously in
Canada by Random House of Canada Limited, Toronto, in conjunction with Disney Enterprises, Inc. This work was originally published by
Golden Books as three separate volumes: *The Flower Prowler*, published in 1998; *The Butterscotch Bandit*, published in 1997;
and *The Dognapper*, published in 1997. RANDOM HOUSE and colophon are registered trademarks of Random House, Inc.
ISBN: 0-7364-2191-2
www.randomhouse.com/kids/disney
First Random House Edition
Printed in the United States of America
10 9 8 7 6 5 4 3 2 1

One spring day Daisy Duck rang Minnie Mouse's doorbell. "Hi, Minnie,"
Daisy said. "I brought you some marigolds from my garden."

"Daisy, you're a dear!" said Minnie. "They'll look perfect with my daffodils."

"Definitely," Daisy agreed. "Daffodils are my favorite flower."

"Mine, too," said Minnie. But when the friends went out to Minnie's
backyard, they had a big surprise.

"My daffodils!" Minnie shrieked. "They're gone!"

"What happened?" Minnie cried. "They were here yesterday!"

"The stems are still here," Daisy pointed out.

Minnie looked more closely. "You're right," she said. "But the flowers are missing. It looks like someone chopped them off with something sharp."

"This is terrible," Daisy said. "It must be a flower prowler!"

"What's this?" Daisy asked a moment later. She pulled a few strands of fuzzy white hair off a bush near the daffodil patch.

"Is it a clue?" Minnie asked. "Maybe the flower prowler left it."

"Maybe," Daisy said. "Or maybe it's from Fluffy's bow."

A moment later Minnie's doorbell rang. Mickey Mouse was standing on the porch. "Hi, Minnie," he said shyly. "I brought you a present." He held out a big bunch of daffodils! And they were tied with a fluffy white ribbon! "Oh, Mickey," Minnie cried. "How could you? You cut down my daffodils!"

"What do you mean, Minnie?" Mickey exclaimed. "I bought these at Power's Flower Shop because I know daffodils are your favorite flowers!"

Minnie smiled. "Really?" she said. She was glad that Mickey wasn't the flower prowler.

Minnie, Daisy, and Mickey decided to look around town for the flower prowler. They headed to the park and found Goofy—with a daffodil in his lapel! And he was playing with a yo-yo that had a fuzzy white string!

"Gawrsh, Minnie," Goofy said. "I didn't do it. This daffodil came from Power's Flower Shop. Mr. Power is having a sale on daffodils today."

"Really?" Minnie said. "That's quite a coincidence."

Daisy nodded. "Maybe we'd better check out Mr. Power's flowers. Right now!"

The four friends went to Power's Flowers. They peeked in the window.

"That's Mr. Power," Mickey said.

Minnie saw that the shopkeeper had a sharp pair of scissors and a fuzzy white mustache. And his shop was full of daffodils!

"He did it!" she cried. "I know it!"

Minnie and her friends burst into the shop. "Where did you get these daffodils?" Minnie asked.

"From a farmer named Mrs. Pote," Mr. Power answered. "She delivers daffodils here every day. But today she brought dozens of extras!"

Minnie wondered if Mrs. Pote could be the prowler. "Where can we find her?" she continued.

Mr. Power pointed. "That-a-way," he said. "You can't miss her. She has fuzzy white hair."

Mrs. Pote's farm was called Pote's Goats. "Yes, I delivered extra daffodils today," Mrs. Pote told Minnie. "My favorite goat, Flower, usually eats a lot of them as soon as they bloom. But today she didn't seem very hungry."

That gave Minnie an idea. "May I see Flower?" she asked.
Mrs. Pote led the friends to a pen. But there was no goat inside!
"Oh, dear!" Mrs. Pote cried. "She must have escaped!"

"Look! There's a hole in the fence," Mickey said, pointing.

"Now what do we do?" Daisy exclaimed. "Not only are Minnie's daffodils gone, but so is Mrs. Pote's goat!"

"Hmmm," said Minnie, deep in thought. "Maybe these two mysteries are connected!"

"What do you mean, Minnie?" Daisy asked.

"I just figured out who the flower prowler might be,"
Minnie explained. "It's someone who really likes daffodils.
Someone who likes them even more than we do!"

Daisy held up the fuzzy strands of hair. "Don't forget this," she reminded Minnie. "Isn't it still a clue?"

"It sure is," Minnie agreed. "And so is this!" She pointed toward a trail of footprints. "Just follow me!"

Minnie and the others followed the footprints straight to Daisy's yard. There was Flower, happily munching away. "See?" Minnie said. "I knew it! There's our flower prowler. Now, if we could only train her to like weeds instead!"

Minnie Mysteries

The Butterscotch Bandit

"Delicious!" Minnie Mouse said, taking a tiny taste of a butterscotch brownie. She had just baked a whole batch of the tasty treats for Daisy Duck's party. "The gang will gobble these up," she said to herself as she wrapped the brownies in tinfoil and tucked the package into a pretty pink shopping bag.

When Minnie arrived at Daisy's house, the other guests were already there. Daisy was taking a platter of food out of the refrigerator while Donald Duck looked on hungrily. Goofy, who was wearing bandages on both thumbs, was carefully petting Mickey Mouse's dog, Pluto.

"I was trying to hang up some pictures," Goofy explained to Minnie. "I sorta missed—twice."

"Gosh, I'm glad you're here, Minnie," Mickey said with a bashful smile. "Would you like to dance?"

"I'd love to," Minnie said as she dropped her shopping bag on the kitchen table and followed Mickey to the living room.

Minnie was still dancing with Mickey half an hour later
when she remembered the treats she had brought.

"The butterscotch brownies!" she exclaimed. "I brought
some for the party, but I forgot to unpack them."

"Well, what are you waiting for?" asked Goofy, smacking
his lips hungrily. "Let's eat!"

Minnie ran to the kitchen. But when she got there, she had a big surprise. The shopping bag was tipped over on the table—and there was nothing inside but some crumbs and tinfoil. Minnie looked all around the kitchen, but the butterscotch brownies were gone!

Minnie went back to the living room. "My brownies are missing!" she cried, waving the empty bag in the air.

"*I* haven't seen them!" said Daisy, Donald, and Mickey, one after the other, as they shook their heads.

Goofy shrugged. "I wish I had," he said sadly. "But I haven't."

"Well, someone must have taken them," said Minnie. "They were in this bag when I got here. One of you must have sneaked out to the kitchen and gobbled down every last bite."

"I didn't take your brownies, Minnie," Daisy said. "I don't even *like* butterscotch."

"Really?" Minnie said. "I didn't know that."

Mickey laughed. "Everybody knows that Daisy would sooner eat spinach than butterscotch," he said.

"Yup," Goofy agreed. "That's why Donald always gets butterscotch sundaes when he goes to the ice cream parlor with Daisy—he knows he won't have to share. That doesn't work when he's with me, though," he added, rubbing his belly.

"I guess that proves *you're* not the thief, Daisy," Minnie said. "So who is?"

"It wasn't me," Mickey said quickly. "You and I have been dancing nonstop since you got here, Minnie. I haven't even been *near* the kitchen."

"That's true," Minnie said. "You couldn't be the butterscotch brownie thief. But if it wasn't you and it wasn't Daisy, then who *was* it?"

Goofy gulped nervously. "I sneaked out to the kitchen once when no one was looking," he admitted. "I even ate a few things. But I didn't touch that bag."

Minnie looked at him thoughtfully. Goofy liked to eat—but did that mean he was guilty?

Then Minnie realized something. "You *couldn't* have done it, Goofy," she said. "How could you unwrap the tinfoil package with both of your thumbs bandaged?"

Goofy held up his thumbs, looking relieved. "Gosh, I couldn't," he agreed.

Donald was looking more and more anxious. When Minnie turned to
him, he squawked, "It wasn't me! It wasn't me!"

Daisy gave him a suspicious stare. "Are you sure, Donald?"

Donald nodded vigorously. "I, um, might have smelled them," he said.
"I even might have unwrapped the tinfoil to take a peek. But I absolutely,
positively, did not taste your brownies—not even one crumb."

Minnie wasn't sure whether or not to believe him. Donald liked to eat almost as much as Goofy did. And he *had* unwrapped the package. Was he telling the whole truth?

Minnie decided to trust Donald. After all, she didn't have any proof that he was the thief.

"Come on," she said. "Let's go comb the kitchen for clues."

The five friends went out to the kitchen and started their search.

Daisy kept peeking nervously at the back door. "If the thief wasn't any of us," she whispered to Minnie, "does that mean a stranger sneaked in and snitched your snacks? That would be scary!"

"Hey, Minnie," called Mickey. "I found some footprints." He pointed at the floor below the table.

"Come on," Minnie cried. "Let's track down our thief!" She and her friends followed the trail of footprints across the kitchen, up the stairs, and into Daisy's bedroom.

The footprints finally disappeared beneath Daisy's bed. Mickey kneeled down and peeked underneath. "Oh, Pluto," he scolded as he pulled out a guilty-looking dog with butterscotch crumbs all over his mouth.

Pluto let out a groan and gave his owner a woeful look.

Minnie just smiled. "Don't be too tough on him, Mickey," she said, giving Pluto a pat on the head. "It looks as if he's already paying for his crime—with quite a tummy ache!"

Minnie Mysteries

The Dognapper

"Minnie!" cried Mickey Mouse over the phone. "I need your help!"

"What's the matter, Mickey?" Minnie Mouse asked.

"I have to be in town in ten minutes for a dentist's appointment, and Goofy promised to play with Pluto while I'm gone. But he hasn't shown up yet, and Pluto is begging for a walk in the park. Can you come over?"

"I'll be there in a jiffy," Minnie promised as she pulled on her coat.

Minnie and Pluto were playing ball in the park when Daisy Duck came along.

"Want to come shopping with me?" Daisy asked Minnie. "There's a super new shoe store on Poteet Street."

"Sorry, but I can't," said Minnie. "I promised Mickey I'd look after Pluto while he's at the dentist. He'll be away at least another half hour."

Daisy smiled. "That's not very long," she said. "I'll wait with you until he gets home." So the friends headed back to Mickey's house.

Suddenly Minnie and Daisy heard a shriek coming from outside.

"Help!" cried a neighbor. "My cat is stuck in a tree!"

Before Minnie or Daisy could reply, the neighbor started dragging them away. "Wait," Minnie cried. "What about Pluto?"

"You mean that dog?" said the neighbor. "He can't come—poor Pussykins will be so terrified that she'll never come down!"

Minnie hesitated. But the neighbor needed them.

"We'll be right back," Minnie promised as she tied Pluto's leash to the trunk of a shady tree. She tested the knot, making sure it was tight enough.

It took only a few minutes to coax Pussykins down from her perch in the tree. But when Minnie and Daisy got back to Mickey's yard, they were met with a dreadful surprise. Pluto was gone!

"But how?" Minnie cried. "He couldn't have unhooked the leash by himself."

Daisy grabbed her friend's arm. "Do you know what this means, Minnie?" she said with a gulp. "Pluto has been dognapped!"

Minnie and Daisy searched the rest of the yard, then hurried up and down the street, questioning everyone they met.

"I just passed a dog," said an elderly man. "He was with a short, stout, grumpy-looking fellow in a red hat."

"It must have been Pluto!" Minnie cried. "Which way did they go?"

The man pointed. "Over that way," he said.

Minnie and Daisy raced down the street. They almost ran right past a man in a red hat, walking a bulldog.

"Daisy, wait," Minnie said, stopping to look again. The man was short and stout. He also looked rather grumpy, possibly because he was grunting and groaning as he tried to get his dog to move.

The man saw Minnie staring at his dog. "He's lazier than mud," he snapped, sounding as grumpy as he looked. "If I didn't drag him out for a walk twice a day, he'd never move a muscle."

"That must be the dog that the old man was talking about," Minnie said to Daisy as the man in the red hat dragged his bulldog away.

"But that's not Pluto," Daisy cried. "Oh, I get it," she said a moment later. "We forgot to describe him. We forgot to say that he's a golden-brown dog."

"Did you say you're looking for a golden-brown dog?" asked a little girl as she tugged on Minnie's sleeve. "I just saw one. He's tied to the mailbox across from the park—over there."

"Thanks a bunch!" said Minnie.

She and Daisy ran toward the park. "This time it's *got* to be Pluto," Daisy cried. "How many golden-brown dogs could there be around here?"

Daisy and Minnie turned the corner and saw the mailbox. Minnie
stopped short. "I think I know the answer to that," she said. "There are
at least *two* golden-brown dogs around here."

A dog was tied to the mailbox. He had golden-brown fur—but he
wasn't Pluto. "Oh, no!" Daisy cried. "Will we *ever* find him?"

Minnie asked a passing mailman if he had seen any dogs.

"I saw a poodle with sharp teeth in the yard on the corner," the mailman said. "Barely escaped with my trousers in one piece. Aside from that, I saw only one other dog. A tall, gangly fellow was walking him."

"Was the dog about this high, with golden-brown fur and a green collar?" Daisy asked, raising her hand to Pluto's height.

The mailman nodded. "That's right. The guy walking him had a big nose and big feet, and he was carrying a purple ball."

"A purple ball!" Daisy exclaimed. "The dognapper not only dognapped Pluto—he stole his toy, too!"

Minnie nodded thoughtfully. "Which way were they walking?" she asked.

"That way," the mailman said, pointing toward the park.

Minnie turned to Daisy. "I think I know who took Pluto," she said. "Come on, let's go!"

Daisy followed Minnie into the park. Sure enough, they soon spotted Pluto, safe and sound. And standing right next to him was—Goofy!

"So, I was right!" said Minnie. "*Goofy* was the dognapper."

Goofy scratched his head and looked bewildered. "Dognapper?" he asked.

"We thought someone had stolen Pluto from Mickey's yard," Minnie said as she gave Pluto a big hug.

"Gawrsh," Goofy said. "Sorry about that. When I saw my little pal tied to that tree, I figured Mickey left him there to wait for me. I promised to look after him, but my watch broke so I was a little late."

"How did you figure out that Pluto was with Goofy?" Daisy asked Minnie.

"I knew a dognapper wouldn't take the ball," Minnie said. "But a dog *walker* would. And when the mailman pointed to the park, I knew I had solved the mystery."

"I get it!" said Daisy, and Goofy nodded.

Pluto barked happily, and Minnie laughed. "I guess that's Pluto's way of saying that three dog walkers are better than one."

Daisy nodded. "And *definitely* better than one dog*napper*!"